A Safe Place

A Nightmare Novella

by N.B. Ventura

DORRANCE PUBLISHING CO
EST. 1920
PITTSBURGH, PENNSYLVANIA 15238

Dorrance Publishing Co
585 Alpha Drive
Pittsburgh, PA 15238
Visit our website at *www.dorrancebookstore.com*

ISBN: 979-8-88729-475-9
eISBN: 979-8-88729-975-4

A Safe Place

A Nightmare Novella

ALAN NOBLE STEPPED OFF THE PLATFORM AT MacArthur Station and onto the B-A-R-T train bound for the SFO airport. He wasn't going to the end of the line - at least not in a literal sense.

The station was nearly empty at this time of night and the train car was desolate. The bare walls of the train's interior, where ambulance-chasing lawyers and Bay Area events were once advertised, made Alan feel even more alone. The train's seats had been removed years ago to make space for the people filed in like sardines during commuting hours. With nowhere to rest, Alan held tightly to the cold, steel bar overhead and looked at his reflection in the window.

He was horrified - but not surprised - by what he saw. All the color had left his face, leaving a pale mask of his usual self. Dark rings – from too many sleepless nights - formed under his bloodshot eyes.

His hands were clammy and kept slipping off the bar as the train jostled to and fro. The hum and whine of the railway would've normally sent Alan into an uncontrollable doze.

Not tonight.

Tonight, Alan felt hyperaware of every little nauseating movement of the train. Every sound he heard was deafening.

Tonight, Alan was doing something he never thought possible. Tonight, he was doing something dangerous, inconceivable - not to mention illegal. The long list of variables that could go wrong flooded back into Alan's mind, but he remained determined.

Alan was not deterred because a little voice in the back of his mind said it was worth it. He had to go on, if for no other reason than to, just this once, *feel* something, to experience something that would give his existence some purpose, some drive, or at least some hedonistic pleasure.

This idea – small but growing more powerful by the mile - was originally not Alan's.

He was a passive man, an introvert working as a mid-level computer analyst. His position afforded him the luxury of blending into the wallpaper. People didn't notice him, which made living that much easier.

Alan, like so many people, did not have friends.

It was too difficult to cultivate friendships when saying the wrong thing could lead to a fine, or worse: jail time.

At Alan's work, everyone kept to themselves. Eye contact was avoided unless absolutely necessary, for the fear that someone could mistake meeting one's gaze thing leering.

Leering was a micro-aggression.

Conversations were unheard of for the same reason. If Alan were to ask, "Where did you go to school?" or, "Did you go to college?" His questions could be interpreted as an expression of his surprise that the person was capable of attending college. The interlocutor could then further perceive that Alan was making such a claim because of his or her race, gender, income, or sexual orientation.

Forming conclusions based on demographics was a micro-aggression.

Two weeks before Alan got on the SFO - bound train, his life of modern seclusion was turned upside down and inside out.

Her name was Sarah.

She started working on the same floor as Alan, and he crossed paths with her in the break room. Alan ventured inside the dingy lounge only to refill his coffee, and one day, standing behind him and politely waiting her turn, was a beautiful woman, smiling benignly.

At first, Alan was horrified that he had made eye contact with her. Then, internally, he systematically chastised himself for thinking that she was beautiful   or, for that matter, assuming that she was, in fact, a "she".

Assumptions about gender were micro-aggressions.

But he then noticed that she was still smiling at him, with the same look of appraisal.

For the first time in a long time, Alan asked a question.

"Are you new here?"

"How observant," she said playfully. She had porcelain skin, with a touch of light freckles spread evenly over her nose and cheekbones. Long hair, the color of rich burgundy, spilled over her shoulders. Her eyes seemed to be in constant conflict over whether they should stay emerald green or ocean blue.

It had been a long time since Alan allowed himself to see someone - really *see* them. He was not in the least bit disappointed.

"Sorry," she continued, "with my dry sense of humor and tendency towards sarcasm, I can come off as rude when I'm trying to be clever."

Alan realized that while he was sizing her up, he wasn't speaking, but instead just staring at her like a deer in headlights, his mouth catching flies.

"No apologies necessary," he finally stammered. "I'm just not used to…"

"I know," she said with a roll of her eyes. "'Speaking is equal to a physical act. Safe speech is a handshake. Hate speech is an assault.'"

Alan was impressed. "You quoted the law perfectly."

She gave him a quizzical smile. "How did you know I quoted it perfectly?"

"Because I develop software concepts. Each proposal has to have a legal disclaimer which must include nothing but Progressive Laws."

"All of them?" she asked as she filled her mug with fresh coffee. He couldn't help but notice that her mug was pink instead of the standard grey. Grey was considered the "safe color" in that it is nearly impossible to offend any Protected Class with grey.

Pink could generate questions involving personal interests. Those questions could be deemed invasive or antagonistic.

Antagonism was a micro-aggression.

"Yes." he answered, "All one hundred and twenty."

She was staring at the corner of the room, obviously thinking, when she asked, "How many times do you think you wrote those laws?"

The question was simple, yet terrible. The answer was nearly unbearable. Alan was an analyst with an academic background entirely saturated in mathematics. His mind computed numbers as simple as his body walked or breathed. Calculations were beyond second nature to him, so though he hated to think of the exact number of times that he had punched in the Progressive Laws, Alan couldn't help but reply with sincere honesty.

"Sadly," he answered, "I have written the Progressive Laws four hundred and eighty thousand times."

The woman – whom he had noted from her nametag – was named "Sarah" gasped and her mouth dropped in sudden disbelief. The creamer packet that she had been gingerly pouring into her pink mug accidentally slipped between her fingers and was instantly submerged into the cup's steaming contents. She instinctively tried to pull out the packet, and after dipping her hand in the cup, she reeled back in and committed a crime.

"Jesus Christ! That was hot!"

It took her a few moments to realize she had just potentially committed an assault on Alan. She looked at him with an apologetic look on her face.

"Don't worry about it-" Alan said. "I'm not religious."

Sarah breathed a sigh of relief. "Oh good. I don't want another citation."

"Another?"

"Yeah, my parents always told me I was too outgoing. It used to get me into a lot of trouble."

"I can imagine," Alan muttered. Sarah began to stir the contents of the rescued creamer into the coffee, changing the aroma in the air from bitter to sweet. Maybe it was the pregnant pause in the conversation or the way Sarah looked intently at her cup as the coffee changed color, but Alan decided to take a risk. "You know, what I *can't* imagine is why anyone would be offended by what you said."

Sarah slowly looked up and cautiously locked eyes with Alan. "How…how do you mean?"

Alan knew perfectly well that he was committing a crime.

Progressive Law # 98: To marginalize the offense is to assault the offended.

Alan, though stepping completely outside of his comfort zone, continued, "I just mean that since you burned yourself, what you said was merely a reaction to that pain. It just seems, I don't know…"

"Ridiculous?" Sarah finished for him.

"Yeah, that about sums it up. 'Ridiculous' is a perfect word for it."

Sarah smiled a contagious, beautiful smile. She then said, "Alan?"

"Yes?"

"Would you like to have lunch together?"

Alan hadn't eaten with any company for years. Since the discussion was nearly prohibited from the table, he found that eating with others was awkward at best, and downright creepy at worst. Yet the idea of spending more time with Sarah seemed almost intoxicating. He would say yes, even if it meant staring at the wall and chewing in silence. "Sure," he said.

"Great." She lifted the cup to her mouth and sipped once, testing its heat. She began to walk away and said casually, "It's a date."

Alan stood for a while staring at the coffee counter, trying to accept what had just happened. He was simultaneously nervous and excited.

Alan was anticipating meeting Sarah at noon in the building's cafeteria, a solemn place, where the sound of silverware and sliding chairs dominated the dreary air. He often, like so many others, preferred to eat in his office to avoid that cryptic quietude.

Before he rose out of his chair to leave, he heard a small tapping at the doorway.

He assumed it was his supervisor giving him a reconfigured quota of programs for the day.

Instead, Sarah walked in. "I hope I'm not too early."

"Not at all," Alan responded, quickly rising out of his chair. "Have a seat, please." As she sat down, he realized that he was still standing. "Sorry, I was just a little startled," he stammered as he sat back down.

"It's okay. I should've warned you how much I can't stand that mausoleum they call a cafeteria."

"To be honest, I can't stand it much, either," he agreed.

Alan noticed that Sarah's Tupperware of salad was also pink. She cracked it open, and Alan braced himself for the usual bizarre silence which pervaded any time he ate with others. Ever one to astound him, Sarah opened her mouth and said, "I'm surprised you didn't cite the Law just a moment ago."

Baffled, Alan asked, "Why would I want to cite the Law?"

"I compared the cafeteria to a mausoleum, isn't that a Progressive crime?"

He then saw that, in fact, it was a crime.

Progressive Law #103: Derogatory comparisons cause offense when stated to any party who finds the subject of comparison laudable.

"You're right," Alan admitted, "but in this case, I happen to agree with you, so it's not an offense."

Sarah stopped eating for a moment and wondered, "What if you were?"

"I don't understand…" Alan began to feel uncomfortable with where this line of questioning was going, yet he found himself simultaneously intrigued. After all, it had been years since Alan had an informal conversation - one that didn't have to do with work or finances, that is.

"What I meant to say," Sarah continued, "is that…suppose you were offended by what I said. Say you liked the cafeteria, so you strongly disagreed with my opinion. What would you do then?"

Alan really thought about the question. After some time he answered honestly, "I wouldn't do anything. I may say I disagree, but that would be the end of it."

"You wouldn't want to go to an S.P. and turn me in?"

That shook him. "Absolutely not!" he exclaimed louder than he meant to.

"Interesting." Sarah mused as she ate some arugula and spinach. "Isn't it true that by openly disagreeing with me, you also broke the Law?"

Again, Alan had to think about the zero tolerance consequences of open disagreements. Then, he reluctantly admitted, "Yes, that is true."

"So, what then?" she asked and set down her plastic container. She looked as though she knew the answer.

"You tell me," Alan challenged.

"I'll gladly tell you." Sarah leaned her elbows on Alan's desk and stared at him with those intense blue-green eyes. "We both would admit each other's offenses to an S.P. warden. Both of us would simultaneously be given sanctuary and cited at the same damn time."

Alan did not see the profanity coming but felt that Sarah's conclusion held enough weight to merit one.

A Safe Place, or "S.P." for short, was a designated zones where victims of micro-aggressions were given sanctuary from the rest of society. Wardens were in charge of supplying victims with every possible comfort, provided that they named their offenders. Equipped with the names of the perpetrators, wardens then called the local Police Department's OLU, or Offensive Language Unit, which had the power to find, cite, and possibly jail the offenders, depending upon the severity of the offense.

"I can tell," Alan began cautiously, "that you have a very strong opinion about Progressive Law."

"How can I not? It seems mad that we can't be honest with each other. Have I harmed you with my opinions?"

"Well, no."

"Then tell me something, Alan. Tell me, how do you feel about the laws that you have had to write and rewrite four hundred and eighty thousand times?"

Alan hated that number, the number that had already grown larger since they had first met that morning. He loathed how well he could parrot those laws. The taste that they left in his mouth was unbearable. Alan looked over at the closed door, then back at the only person in his office.

For a moment he hesitated, then firmly said, "I fucking hate them."

Sarah looked flabbergasted. Her eyes went wide with disbelief, as though she hadn't properly heard the words that were just uttered or comprehended the venomous tone that came with them. "Is that true Alan?"

"…yes," he answered head down, facing his desk.

"Thank God," Sarah started to laugh. It wasn't a mocking laugh. It was pretty, ringing like bells above a churchyard. It rang out through the room, across his desk, and into his soul.

Suddenly, Alan began to laugh too. He felt liberated by every chortle. After so many years of internalizing his true feelings, he felt a tremendous sense of catharsis having expressed himself honestly to a person who miraculously felt the same way about the Revolution and its stupid Progressive Laws.

After the laughter died down, Sarah said, "Look, I got to run. Let's have lunch tomorrow?"

"Yes, why not?"

"Who knows?" she joked as she opened the door, "maybe tomorrow you will eat something."

It was only when the door closed that Alan realized he never touched his lunch.

After that fateful morning, Sarah and Alan had lunch every day. At first, they took baby steps in their conversations, starting with the weather, then work. But eventually, they dove into real topics. They talked about the Revolution and about Progressive Law.

Sarah told Alan about how speech used to be so free, people would stand on a stage for a living in order to tell jokes designed to offend people. People wouldn't get upset; they would instead pay to attend.

They talked about how movies and books used to depict all manners of violence and foul language. People would stand in line and pay good money for the privilege of that sort of entertainment.

The more they discussed and exchanged stories, the more resentful Alan became of the world around him. He felt bound and gagged. Being unable to truly express himself without fear of losing everything was like drowning in quicksand, the more he resisted, the worse he felt.

He craved more than just their discussions.

They were sitting in his office, as usual, talking about all the manners of things, when he blurted, "Enough talk, let's go…do something."

Sarah stopped speaking mid-sentence and asked, "What do you mean?"

"Well, we always say that 'this book', or 'that film' exists. So, let's go find that book so we can read it. Let's track down that movie, and for God's sake, watch it!" Profanity and the use of censored language were coming easier to him now. He felt like a different person after meeting Sarah. Pandora's Box had been opened by their meeting, and it could never again be shut.

"Are you serious?"

"Yes."

"What you're suggesting," Sarah began, "is considered treason. If we were caught…If we were caught, they wouldn't just cite us, or jail us-"

"I know."

"Then you're clearly insane," she said, both playful and concerned.

"I'm not insane. I feel like I'm suffocating. I'm a prisoner in my own country, trying desperately to see the light between the bars."

"Now you're a poet?"

Alan looked down, his face turning a dark crimson. "Forget it," he said, in more of a snarl than a voice.

Sarah touched his hand across the desk. He felt her smooth palm and tiny, elegant fingers caress his knuckles.

"Alan, I'm sorry. I was trying to make light of the topic. I warned you, I'm a bit of a smart-ass."

"That's true." Alan tentatively looked up at her. "Don't tell me you've never thought of it."

"Of course, I have. Since I was a young girl, I thought about finding the contraband that I heard adults talking about. I once heard my parents mention a book about a spider and a pig who were friends. I've wanted to get my hands on it ever since."

"When I was young, I heard of a banned film about a group of kids searching for pirate treasure. Apparently, they were being chased by adults who wanted it for themselves. It was called 'The Goonies', I think. But I can't be certain."

"Can you imagine how much fiction - how much art - there used to be?"

"There seemed to be an endless variety before the Revolution. Surely there must be some left."

"That's true," Sarah pondered. "The book burnings, the film burnings, and the art burnings were all done by mobs of outraged people who dubbed themselves 'Social Justice Warriors'. It only makes sense that some people did the opposite. During the Revolution, some groups could've gone to great lengths to stow away offensive artifacts. When the Revolution ended and the Progressive Social Justice Department was established, the authorities assumed that all censored material was either destroyed or in their possession."

After Sarah finished, Alan sprang from his chair. He opened his office door only slightly, to see if anyone was listening. The hallway was a ghost town; no one could be seen or heard. He quietly shut the door and began to thoughtfully pace the length of his office.

"What are you thinking about?"

"I'm sorry Sarah, I don't wish to frighten you, but if there's a group out there who are holding on to offensive artifacts, I need to find them. I need to experience what makes life worth living, rather than live a false life from a safe place. Every day I wake up, shower, come to work, go home, eat dinner, and stare at a fucking wall!"

"I understand, Alan," Sarah said soothingly. "When I met you, I knew you wanted more than what was allowed. You wanted to feel, to think, to laugh and cry."

Alan noticed something change in Sarah's voice and demeanor. Her bubbly, positive nature disappeared. What remained was a cold, intelligent voice with a touch of compassion.

She continued, "I saw you from a distance long before you ever noticed me. You seemed like a man struggling with a chain around his neck; constricted from thought, fearing every word that came out of your mouth. You are a psychological slave, ruled by thought wardens that demand absolute obedience. I, however, am free."

"Who are you, really?" Alan wondered, taken aback by her confession.

"Have a seat, Alan."

He crossed the room and sat down, once again staring into those exquisite eyes, this time, with a whole new appreciation and trepidation. "I'm waiting," he said.

"I, and others like me, are called Keepers."

"Keepers…" Alan said inquisitively. "Keepers of offensive artifacts?"

"In one way, yes, but there's more to it than that. I am charged with keeping certain offensive artifacts and passing them down in secret to those who are willing to experience them. But I also keep something else. You see, the items you wish to seek out are mere representations of what once existed. A knowledge of ethics, if you will."

"Ethics?" Alan asked, confused, "You mean S.J.E?"

"No, not Social Justice Ethics. What the system hasn't told you, Alan, is that there was – and still exists - a way in which people could argue about the most illegal subjects, by today's standards, and neither party would be traumatized. It is that wisdom, the knowledge of ethics, that I, and so many others like me in this new world order, have been tasked to keep safe and hold true."

"I don't fully understand," Alan shamefully admitted.

"How can you, when all you know is the material you can lawfully access?" Sarah stood up slowly and pulled out a card. She slid it across his desk. "I have to go now, Alan. My work here is finished. The next step is entirely up to you."

"To me?"

"Yes. You can forget about me and our little conversations if you wish. Our friendship will end, and you can go back to staring at your living room wall. Or you can pick up that card. Follow the instructions printed on it, and perhaps our friendship will truly begin. Either way, Alan, I wish you well."

She opened the door and began to leave when Alan stopped her.

"Wait a minute, I'll still see you at work."

Sarah gave him a sad smile. "I've never worked here. I simply followed you inside. It's one of the only benefits of living in a society that is terrified to ask questions." She then disappeared down the hallway, leaving Alan completely speechless.

Though he had already memorized the writing on the card, Alan pulled it out of his pocket and read it all over again:

The B.A.R.T. train stopped at an underground station. The conductor screeched through the overhead speakers, "Powell Street Station. This is an SFO- bound train-"

Alan stepped onto the platform, looking guilty and hunted. He ascended the stairs leading to the frigid, open air of San Francisco and walked down Market Street. There were few cars and even fewer lights. Though he had heard the signs and shops that once lived on this street used to burst with color, now, he only saw dark and empty buildings slowly imploding from years of decay.

Bolted to those buildings and facing every street corner were weather-resistant communication screens. Inside them sat built-in sound systems whose announcements penetrated every doorway and alley.

Alan stopped for a moment to see what the government was broadcasting today. The screen displayed footage of "offenders" being dragged into the back of police trucks. They obviously had been meeting to discuss illegal subjects. The narrator's androgynous voice explained that the group had been infiltrated by a now-traumatized citizen. The screen panned over to a woman who sobbed uncontrollably, her chest heaving and hands convulsively shaking. Due to the citizen's tragic assault, she would be granted permanent asylum in a Safe Place.

Progressive Law #33: Those convicted of aggression are to be treated with any and all conceivable forms of aggression by the Children of the Revolution.

Alan knew that if he was caught tonight, he would end up like those on the screen. He knew their fate. They would never be set free if the victim was placed in permanent protection. They would be convicted without trial and become Title One Recanters.

Recanters were forced to serve victims in Safe Places. Title Three Recanters were there for a very short period. Title Twos were convicted for up to ten years. Title Ones, however, served for life. They were considered the worst offenders because they had recruited others to engage in offenses with them.

The idea of being enslaved to spineless creatures like the woman blubbering on the communication screen sent a chill down Alan's spine. He decided at that moment that if he were to be caught tonight, he would find a way to kill himself.

He turned away from the screen and made a left onto Powell Street. The street was even more desolate than Market Street. Nearly all of Powell Street had been evacuated after massive riots. Alan recalled that it used to be a pocket of racist poison called "Chinatown". Alan couldn't remember if the Chinese had been forced to live there, or if there was some historical significance involving early immigration. What he did know was that during the Revolution, any place that gave favoritism to race or class was evacuated and destroyed. They were then sanitized by the locals who, whipped into a frenzy of Social Justice, destroyed the very neighborhoods they were once proud to live in.

Alan stopped again as he came upon what looked like a creature from a storybook, holding up a destroyed archway. It appeared to be made of stone or at least was simply designed to look that way. Such liberated creativity was completely alien to Alan, and he was mesmerized by its flawlessness in the midst of shattered concrete and exposed rebar.

"It was once known as the Dragon Gate," said a male voice behind him.

Alan nearly jumped a foot into the air and swiftly turned, expecting a police officer with a submachine gun.

Instead, he found an old man with a cane. The man had a large, brown beard and a military-style coat. He wore a wide-brimmed fedora that seemed older than he was.

"I didn't mean to frighten you, young man," the old man apologized. "I say 'young man' because that is how I perceive you in the context of our species and society. Are you offended?" The man leaned on his cane and his eyes, like daggers, pierced into Alan's, awaiting a response.

Alan, still recovering from the shock of the old man's presence, finally said, "No, I am not offended."

"No, of course not. How could someone who is crazy enough to wander down the Powell Street Evac Zone and smile at a dragon be offended by anything so humdrum as 'young man'?"

"I wasn't smiling, was I?"

"Not on the outside," said the old man with a smirk. "Now, what is your name?"

"Noble."

"Oh, and humble, too."

"No, no. Noble's my last name-"

"Merely a joke, Noble," the man said with a chuckle. "You will learn that when you join us: a sense of humor is crucial."

"Then you're a…Keeper."

"Yes," the old man confirmed. "Though my parents named me years ago, I now go by the name the Keepers have granted me. I am called Uriel. We've been expecting you, Alan."

"Sarah spoke with you, then?"

"If that is the name she gave you, then yes, Sarah spoke with me. Now, shall we?" He pointed his cane towards the darkness of the street.

Alan walked with him in silence until Uriel began making small talk.

"My job, you see," Uriel said, "is to keep watch at the gate for men and women such as yourself."

"Why is that your job?" Alan asked, genuinely curious.

"One simple reason: I'm old," Uriel laughed. "I had many jobs throughout the years, but these days I'm not as quick as I used to be."

"So, they leave you out here alone, in the dark? What if something happens? What if I'm not who I appear to be, and my whole purpose is to turn everyone in? What then?"

Uriel stopped walking and slowly turned to look at Alan. His face was no longer kind and feeble. Underneath his grandfatherly veneer was a cold, hard man: a man who could kill him without a second thought. Alan wondered about the sights that Uriel had seen, and the other jobs he had done to keep the truth protected.

In a flash, the deadly look left Uriel's face, and the happy old man returned with a sly, impish grin. "I may be slower, but I still have my talents."

Alan was beginning to wonder what he had gotten himself into.

The ruins of Saint Mary's Church were unlike anything Alan had ever seen. The meeting place was like an ancient stone castle whose curtain walls were breached long ago, its former stained-glass windows now shattered and boarded up. Yet, the closer Alan looked at the church, the more he saw the damage was mostly superficial.

"That's as far as I go," Uriel said. "I have to keep watch."

"Alright…" Alan whispered as he gazed cautiously into the dark mouth of the church's doorway. He felt a gentle, but strong hand grip his shoulder. He turned to look at Uriel.

"It's all right, Alan. You've made it this far. The hardest part of your journey was recognizing the path. Now," Uriel looked at the church, "you're at the end of it."

All Alan could think to say was, "Thank you."

Uriel remained silent but squeezed Alan's shoulder before walking back to the Dragon Gate.

Alan watched him disappear into the darkness before slowly creeping up the broken steps leading to the entrance of Saint Mary's.

When he got to the door, he saw that it was still solid. He knocked on the wood. The sound of his knuckles hitting the door seemed deafening, and the steps seemed to quake as if it were a sin to make noise.

At first, nothing happened. Alan stared at the door for what seemed like ages, when at last he heard several bolts slide back in unison, and the door slowly sank inward. He didn't know what to expect. He briefly wondered if he would find a group of old men and women, wizards and witches, keeping the ancient magic alive. Or perhaps this was all some government plot to capture Progressive criminals.

What he didn't expect was a man in a red sweater vest, smoking a cigar.

"Hello, Alan. Glad you could make it," the man said with a huge smile. "Welcome to paradise."

The man reached out his right hand to shake Alan's. Alan accepted and while they shook hands, the man pulled him into the church. He then put his arm on Alan's shoulder, as if they were lifelong friends.

"My name's Milton. I'll give you the grand tour."

Alan didn't know how to react to such informality: the eye contact, the handshaking, the arm around the shoulder. Since making his way onto Powell Street, Alan had experienced more broken laws than he could count.

"Don't worry," Milton said. "It's going to take time to get used to how things are around here."

"It is certainly surprising."

Alan looked to the left of the entrance and saw a man armed with an assault rifle, and wearing military-grade armor. Behind the guard, he could see that someone had turned what was once a confessional into a crude communication center. A man inside spoke rapidly into a headset in a coded language as he swiveled on a chair, splitting his attention between several computer screens.

"That's Hermes. He's always in communication with the other cells."

"Other cells? You mean there are Keepers in other places?"

"Oh, yes. We cannot risk being all in one place." Milton escorted Alan to the main doors, leading to the church proper. When he opened them, a cacophony of noise hit Alan like a tidal wave. There was a group of people listening to the music of some kind in one corner of the room, while others watched a movie in the other. The film was most certainly contraband: it featured a man in a tie, dancing and cutting off another man's ear. The scene was brutal and seemingly pointless. It should have shaken him to his very foundation. Instead, he couldn't help but be mesmerized by the action and music. All at once, Alan suddenly discovered that art, no matter how it is portrayed, cannot truly harm you. Even the repulsion that he felt for the scene was itself, entertaining.

"That's a very old film. 'Reservoir Dogs', I believe it is called," Milton said.

"How old is it?"

Milton shrugged, "I'm not sure. I'd say at least 60 years old, if not more. It's hard to tell with certain relics. Some are fairly recent; others would need a lot of investigation to discover their approximate age."

Alan and Milton moved along. As they did, they saw two people standing several feet apart with an audience of ten or so in front of them. One would speak about an issue and, with passion, argue a point. Then, that person stands quietly and lets their companion speak on the same topic. Both made emotional appeals to the audience to turn them against the other person's opinion. Neither appeared angry, and the audience sat quietly, observing the argument with fascination.

"What is happening here?" Alan inquired in disbelief that people would find entertainment in an argument riddled with micro-aggressions.

"It's not really an argument in the way that you understand it," Milton explained. "The two standing are having a debate."

"They must hate each other, to be so opposed on an issue."

Milton failed to hold back a smile when he said, "This may come as a surprise to you, Alan, but neither of them cares at all about the issue they are debating."

"But…" Alan responded, waving his hands in the air. He couldn't fathom why two people would want to go through such a trial of aggression and assault if they didn't believe what they were saying.

"This will be difficult to explain, but try and follow me, Alan." Milton saw that his cigar had gone out. He took out a match and lit the end, puffing vigorously. He then continued, "You see, Alan, they are engaging in a debate to build their argumentative skills. Without those skills, there would be no understanding that each side has an underlying agreement of goodwill. Under that agreement, anyone can argue anything and find no cause to feel endangered."

What Milton said went against everything Alan had learned as a child. He was taught from a very young age that he, Alan Noble, was a child of the Social Justice Revolution: the Revolution that cleansed and sanitized a corrupt and violent nation of racism, classism, and sexism. The movement eliminated all forms of discrimination by making all people, regardless of their natural existence, victims. He had learned that, in the beginning, there were certain people who were believed to hold all of society's power, but the identity of those people became obscured over time as all races, cultures, and genders merged into a single social monolith. To debate anything in such a uniform society was unthinkable.

Alan knew he was committing treason.

He swayed a little, nearly fainting when Milton caught him by the shoulders.

"It's all right, Alan, no one is being harmed here. We're all friends."

"It's just…just…"

"I know; too much, too soon."

Milton did not speak those words, but Alan didn't have to turn around to know who did. He knew that voice very well.

It was Sarah, walking down from the altar. She looked the same, yet somehow changed, her gait different than before. As she came closer others gave her room, out of respect.

Alan then understood.

She was in charge.

"Sarah," Alan said with a sigh. "It's good to see you again."

"Good to see you, too, Alan," Sarah responded with a glimmer of that former personality he had enjoyed in his office.

She turned to Milton. "Why does he look like he's about to keel over? Did you take him through the back?"

Milton sheepishly responded, "No, I took him through the front. I thought it would be best that he gets a crash course in how we operate."

"Well," she said, obviously agitated, "see that the 'crash course' isn't fatal. In fact," she took Alan's hand and held it, "I'll take over from here."

"As you wish." Milton waved them off before taking a seat to watch the ongoing debate.

"Come with me," Sarah instructed. She grasped Alan's hand and walked to another part of the church.

Alan felt her hand relax as she moved her fingers between his. He felt her warmth radiate through him and couldn't stop beaming when she looked at him with a beautiful and confident smile.

Alan knew then that he loved her.

"Sarah?"

"Yes."

"Why me?"

"I would say it's random, but that's not quite accurate. We have cells in Evac Zones throughout the country. We recruit, by patrolling the nearby cities and looking for those who are about to break down."

"You were spying on me?"

Sarah's hand slipped out of his. She crossed her arms and said flatly, "We were watching for those who kept their heads down as they walked, who looked as though they were on the verge of crying or screaming – those who gazed at their reflections in a window on the street and hated everything they saw."

"You're claiming that was me?"

"No," she said. "That *is* you Present tense, Alan. Can you honestly deny that?"

Alan searched within himself to find the answer, though he knew it well.

"You should know better than anyone, Sarah, how I loathe what I have to endure, day in and day out. I suppose in many ways I began to hate myself. Every time I wrote a Progressive Law, it felt like a part of me was dying."

"We find people like you and see where their loyalties lie. Then, we determine if they are willing to, as you put it Alan, 'do something about it'."

There was a silence between them. Since he entered Saint Mary's, there had been so much to process: the music, the film, the debate, the obscene speech mingled with laughter that seemed to fill the entire church and reverberate from the flying buttresses.

"I am sorry about Milton," Sarah continued. "He was raised in an Evac Zone, so he doesn't get how much of a shock all of this can be. Here," she said, showing him to a back room. "I want to show you what we were once like."

They walked into what Alan would assume was the church's rectory. Sarah opened the door, and what lay inside was more astounding than any open argument.

"This," Sarah said, "is the Room of Relics."

Inside were movie posters of films called, *Star Wars* and *Casablanca*. There were stacks of books, with names like *1984*, *The Old Man and the Sea*, *The Martian Chronicles*, Plato's *Dialogues*, and *Napalm and Silly Putty*, among others. There were signs on the wall that said *Coca-Cola*, *Pepsi-Cola*, *Arby's*, *Comics and More*, *We Buy Gold*, *Adult Arcade Inside*, and many other strange phrases. On the Communication Screen in the middle of the room, a man spoke vigorously against Social Justice. He exclaimed that the entire concept was a game of power that would lead to the destruction of humankind. He argued that post-modernism is not a respecter of any culture or class; its premise was instead to nullify unique skills and talents to focus solely on one's natural existence. "Differences," the man stated, "are what makes us special. We must protect them at all costs.

The interviewer asked how we, as a people, could do just that.

The man responded that everyone should look inward to discover what truly makes them unique, and then imagine a future where all anyone cares about is fear of offending others: a place where political correctness reigns supreme and discourages these differences. "Ask yourself," the man passionately expounded. "In that world, can I ever truly be an individual? Could I ever really stand out, when I do something exceptional, or will I be perceived as a person with privilege grabbing power from others? If post-modernism, Social Justice Warriors, and those that profit from today's ideology get what they truly want, then I predict that within the next generation, we won't be able to recognize the difference between free speech and physical violence."

Alan was enraptured.

No one had ever clearly articulated what Alan had felt for so many years. He had never heard anyone utter the logic that he harbored himself, an ideology in constant conflict with everything he had been taught as a child.

"Who is this man?" Alan asked.

"He was a Canadian professor. This was one of his last interviews. He made it his life's mission to stop the tide of post-modernism, but in the end, it drowned him out."

"What happened to him?"

"We're not entirely sure, but he was likely executed during the Progressive Purges, early in the Revolution. Or he became one of us and hid in the Evac Zones under an assumed name. We'll never truly know."

Alan spent hours talking to the Keepers. He soon learned that their group first formed when the Progressive Laws were ratified, shortly before the Revolution. They spoke freely about all subjects and their knowledge of the world far surpassed Alan's limited understanding. They discussed politics, religion, love, war, hate, and the meaning of existence - and no one feared differing viewpoints. No one was damaged by opposing ideas. Even when the conversations turned contentious, there was always an air of respect between them.

"Sarah, I should probably leave now. It's very late," Alan said, pulling himself from the hundredth fascinating conversation he had overheard that day.

"Leave?" Sarah asked, perplexed. "And go where?"

"Go home."

"Ah, I see, back to the wall that you stare at. Back to your grey chair, your grey bedsheets, and your grey life." As she spoke, the whole church went quiet.

Everyone stared at Alan and Sarah.

"You're not suggesting I live here? Leave my life entirely?"

"What life?"

Alan knew he should have been offended, but there was nothing in his life worth defending. He had nothing but a grey life. No color, no passion, no feeling of accomplishment.

"Alan," Sarah said, "you can leave that strait-jacket of a life and liberate yourself here. With us."

"Do I really have a choice?" he cautiously wondered.

"Of course, Alan. Leave if you wish. No one will stop you."

Alan turned, willing himself to walk past the debaters, past the music and the movie lovers, the guard and Hermes, past Uriel and the Dragon Gate. Back to the train, back to the apartment, back to the job, with its endless code…

He couldn't do it. Though some primal part of him feared staying with the Keepers for one more second, he couldn't bring himself to return home.

He was already home.

With herculean effort, he muttered, "I'll stay."

With those two words came a thunderous applause, that seemed to shake the old stone walls to their core.

Alan smiled, turned back to Sarah, and felt hot tears stream down his face.

She smiled back, a genuine Sarah smile. A smile that reassured him that the sky would not fall, the earth would keep spinning, and he was safe.

The Keepers crowded around Alan and shook his hand. They patted him on the back, while some hugged him and kissed his cheeks. He had never felt more exhilarated and terrified.

Then the alarm sounded.

Sarah's congenial smile transformed into a soldier's coolness. She marched past Alan while he followed in tow.

She stopped at Hermes' communication station.

"What is it?" she demanded.

"It's the O.L.U. They've found us."

Sarah's back straightened and she turned with trepidation as she calmly spoke to the Keepers. "They are coming. Uriel will fight them off for a short time, but eventually, he'll be overrun."

Alan remembered the hardness in Uriel's face and wondered how many O.L.U. officers he would take with him.

Sarah continued, "We are now commencing Operation Northmen."

With that, Keepers of all ages and sizes became a military unit and sprang into action. Each obviously had a role to fulfill, a mission to accomplish.

Milton sent out the last broadcast from Saint Mary's, "*Paradise lost*, I repeat, *paradise lost*."

After the last transmission, Hermes destroyed all the equipment in the communication station by spraying it with a corrosive acid. Other Keepers were meanwhile taking flight in all directions, fleeing the church with assigned relics that were likely to be hidden away in another Evac Zone.

Alan's adrenaline kept him from collapsing into a panic.

He followed Sarah on instinct as she fled through the rectory. They returned to the Room of Relics, its walls and shelves now emptied of their precious contents. Sarah lifted a throw rug off the floor. Beneath it was a trap door, clearly made when the Keepers arrived.

Sarah struggled to get it open.

Alan moved her aside and with both hands, manage to crack open the trap door. A musty odor fled the dark chasm and penetrated his sinuses. He struggled through a coughing fit as Sarah spoke to him.

"Look, you need to stay close to me. We need to get to Pier 33. It's dark, but the O.L.U. has lights and guns, so we'll have to move fast."

"Okay."

Without another word, she dived down into the pit. Alan waited a moment, thought of that grey wall one more time, then dropped into the hole.

He didn't drop far. As soon as he felt his feet hit the floor, a hand grabbed his wrist in the dark. It guided him through what must have been an old sewer system. Alan could tell Sarah knew where she was going. They never stopped, though occasionally she would push him left or right to avoid dangers he couldn't see.

Without warning, he felt Sarah come to a stop.

"Quietly now…" she whispered.

He heard a small click. The damp air in the tunnel faded away and was replaced by the salty spray of the ocean.

Alan detected a door slowly sliding open.

Her hand no longer guided him as the light started to penetrate the opening of the cavern. The illumination quickly became an intense, artificial beam that cast a ghostly filter on everything.

Alan recognized that they were on the Embarcadero; the piers were just across the street.

He followed Sarah to a trellis of ivy next to a fence. She signaled impatiently for him to stay low. When he did, he saw the silhouette of her head nod in approval.

Alan didn't know what they were waiting for, but he certainly didn't like what he saw.

There were wardens patrolling on foot at the entrance of every pier. Spotlights and manned gun towers stood every two hundred feet. As he was making this assessment, an armored personnel carrier sped by, its mounted cameras and a gunner poised and ready out of the top hatch.

Sarah crouched next to Alan and whispered, "We have to make it to Pier 33."

"That's madness," he muttered back. Sweat dripped down his face in defiance of the ocean breeze.

"Just wait for the signal. You won't miss it," she instructed in a cool tone. "When we make our move, follow right behind me and don't stop. Understand?"

He nodded his head. He couldn't believe how calm she was.

Alan started to play out the different scenarios in his mind, and he couldn't imagine one that didn't involve him laid out in the middle of the street, riddled with bullets and soaked in blood.

He really needed to find a restroom.

Alan stayed next to her for what seemed like an eternity. In the pale light, he saw Sarah's obscured features intently watching the structured, routine pacing of the police. For a moment, she looked down and pulled something out of her jacket. It was a metal parcel the size of a pack of cigarettes.

"Here," she said. "I want you to have this."

"What is it?"

"It's a fireproof box. Inside are the directions to the rallying point. Charon should know the way, but in case something happens, you'll know where to go."

"Charon?"

"A Keeper," she said, her breathing getting heavy in preparation for something. "He's waiting for us on a small ship called the 'Styx'."

"What about you, don't you need this?" Alan offered, holding out the box.

"No, I memorized it some time ago. This was always a possibility. Just remember: Pier 33, the *Styx*, Charon is the captain. Understand?"

Alan started to shake with fear. He knew that she was preparing him for the flight of his life. His knees felt like rubber, his head swam, and he sensed every change in the air, every imperfection in the road. Everything was heightened, but nothing seemed real.

"Sarah…" he began. As he looked at her, love and terror merged into an unspeakable emotion.

Alan felt the concussion of the blast before he heard it. When he did, the noise was an unnatural rending of steel and stone, ripping apart in a violent explosion. He didn't need to turn around to know that Saint Mary's was now an annihilated heap of rubble and ashes.

Once they recovered from the shock, Sarah grabbed him by the collar and drew him to her. Time seemed to freeze as their lips pressed together, locking in unity what Alan had missed his entire life.

As soon as it was, it was no more. Sarah broke away and screamed, "Move!"

Her voice, like the starting pistol of an Olympic race, set Alan in motion. He stared at her back, trying not to focus on being gunned down like an animal.

Yet, against all odds, they were making it clear across the Embarcadero. He dared to shoot a glance to his right and left and saw the faces of the guards in the streets and the towers seemingly hypnotized by the ball of fire in the distance.

They were clear across the street and onto the Pier when he heard, "Hey, you!"

Alan nearly stopped, but then he saw that Sarah kept her same pace. The heavy footsteps following in close pursuit reminded him to keep moving.

A small, white boat rested in the water. Its engine already started and its cleats were unhitched. The word, *Styx*, was visible on its aft.

He was almost there, so close he could practically feel his feet hit the deck of the ship.

Shots were fired behind him. His body convulsed in horror as each shot rang out.

Sarah began to slow in front of him but kept moving towards the *Styx*.

In front of them, a flash of muzzle fire and the crack of an automatic assault rifle flew over their heads. Both Sarah and Alan hit the ground hard.

Alan looked behind him. To his surprise, he saw three lifeless policemen splayed out like armored ragdolls.

"C'mon!" a man standing in the wheelhouse of the boat beckoned. He was wearing a black slicker and galoshes and hefting a military rifle in his hands.

Alan jumped back into motion and nearly tripped over Sarah, who was slowly lurching towards the *Styx*. Alan tossed her right arm around his shoulder, and he held her as they jumped onto the ship.

"Charon, get it moving!" Sarah said between ragged breaths.

"I'm on it," the man in the slicker said. He entered the wheelhouse and in seconds, Alan felt the boat break away from the pier.

"Sit me down, please."

Alan sat Sarah down on an aft-facing bench. When they separated, Alan's hands felt sticky and wet.

They locked eyes. There was no need to say anything. He sat down next to her.

Holding hands, the pair watched the fire blazing in the distance grow smaller. They sailed deeper into the bay, the cold cutting through their clothes, drying their tears and Sarah's blood.

Alan was not sure if Sarah died the moment their hands touched, or a few minutes later.

What he did know, was that the person who gave his life meaning, the person he loved without knowing her true name, the savior of what soul still existed within him, was dead.

He reached for the box in his pocket. His fingers felt its square edges through the fabric and he knew it was safe. In time, he would make sure Charon knew where the rallying point was, but for now, he wanted to hold her hand.

Alan continued to hold her hand as the fire of Saint Mary's turned into an undefined cinder in the distance.

He held her, never knowing her name.